It Could

Happen To

Your Child!

Other Books by
Lorraine M. Harris

Sunday Golf Series

Sunday Golf
After Bowling
Golf Course View

Casserole Parade Series

Casserole Parade
Casserole Surprise

Other Books

Not the Norm, A Small Town Story
Intuition (co-author, Deborah Seibert)

For additional information about Lorraine and her books, visit her website, www.lorrainemharris.com

DEDICATION

Lamont, Nicole and Natalie are my source of energy and inspiration. I could not do what I do without their unconditional love and support.

ACKNOWLEDGEMENTS

I want to acknowledge my Lord and Savior because with him I am able to do what I do.

Proverbs 16:1-3, "People make plans in their minds, but only the Lord can make them come true. Depend on the Lord in whatever you do and your plans will succeed."

Shirley Keeney, thank you for taking the time to read my book during its development. She was asked because of her law enforcement experience as a former Baltimore, Maryland Police Officer. The suggestions she offered were helpful and caused me to make changes that made a difference. Shirley's ideas, wisdom, expertise and feedback made the stories more believable.

A big "thank you" to Russell (Russ) and Jo Jones and their guests who listened to me read the stories from this book. Their kindness, thoughtfulness, and candid discussion provided me with insight when writing the discussion questions after each story. Russ, your experience as a Baltimore, Maryland Elementary School Principal, encouraged me to have this book published.

Producing an error-free manuscript is difficult, even with expert review and advice. Words cannot express how grateful I am for Gloria (Gigi) Hey for providing me with candid feedback during the development of this book. I also owe my gratitude and thanks to Marjorie (Marj) McEntyre and Jo Jones for their editing and proofing expertise. To my daughter Natalie Harris, thank you for your time, feedback and ideas.

As always, I take full responsibility for all mistakes and liberties I might have taken.

FOREWARD

In today's high-tech, fast paced society parents are finding difficulty in communicating with their children. However, during these times, more so than ever before, children are often targeted and lured into situations that sometimes lead to abduction or worse.

To validate my concerns, I researched the Internet, and talked to police officers and educators. I was shocked to learn that about 800,000 children go missing every year in the United States. The reasons vary, but many disappearances happen because children do not always understand when they are in danger.

When our lovely daughters were growing up, my husband and I had many discussions with them about a variety of situations. Despite our warnings, we did not realize how unclear we were about who might cause them danger or in what form the danger might occur.

For example, we told our daughters not to talk to *"strangers."* Yet, we encouraged them to speak to someone whom neither, we nor our children knew.

At that moment, we had no idea we had caused them confusion and possible danger. The implication was, it was okay for them to speak to a *"stranger"* when they were with us.

The concern is, *"Would our daughters, think this person was a stranger when they were not with us?"* We began asking ourselves how many times had we confused our children when it came to their well-being?

The media have done an outstanding job in having psychologists, law enforcement officers and other similar professions raise the awareness of how children can be deceived and lured into unsafe situations. The problem is that during the discussions, the same types of examples (such as, cats, dogs, candy, etc.) are given to demonstrate what perpetrators may use to entice children.

Every day, there are more and more situations occurring that make it difficult for children to understand the danger they are in. This is the reason I wrote this book of short stories. The circumstances described happen daily, but don't always cause parents to think twice about their child being at risk.

The stories are meant to help adults and children discuss circumstances that may pose possible threats. After each story, a set of questions are provided to encourage discussions.

Lorraine M. Harris

Table of Contents

KINDERGARTEN TO FIFTH GRADE

1

THE CANDY MAN

The bell rang, ending the school day. The girls and boys of the fourth grade hurried out of the classroom.

Lee Hardy was passing Mrs. Wilson, the teacher's desk, when she stopped him.

He glanced at his teacher, but didn't like her sour lemon pucker face expression. Speaking, her voice was stern.

"Before you leave I need to talk to you."

Lee opened his mouth, but the tone of Mrs. Wilson's words made him remain quiet. He thought about how he needed to go. If he didn't hurry his buddies would leave him. He didn't want to walk home alone.

"Lee, you're one of my best students, but I'm disappointed in you." He listened, staring down at his shoes, not making eye contact with her.

"The last two weeks, I've given you several warnings." She shook her head. "Lee, you've given me no choice. Tonight, I'm calling your parents and telling them how you make noises and throw objects at students while they're working on their class assignments."

She paused. "Do you have anything to say?"

Lee fidgeted and whined, "I finish my work before the other kids and I don't have anything to do."

Mrs. Wilson pursed her lips. "That's no excuse. Several times, I told you to read a book or work on your homework assignments. You have ignored all my suggestions."

Lee wanted to defend his behavior, but instead he pleaded, "I need to leave or I'll be late."

"Go ahead, but I'm calling your parents, tonight. Run along and have a good evening."

He puckered his lips and thought. "How can I have a good evening when you're going to call my parents? Before they hear my side of the story, they'll punish me."

Opening the school's front door, Lee bolted through it. He glanced around. A few girls and boys stood on the sidewalk in front of the school, but none of them were his buddies.

Lee began walking home when a loud clap of thunder sounded. He glanced up and saw the dark clouds looming overhead. Off in the distance a flash of lightning lit up the sky. He pouted, remembering the last words his mother said before he left for school. "Lee, make sure you take your raincoat. It's supposed to rain today."

He mumbled. "Great!" He had forgotten his raincoat and by the time he gets home, he'll be wet. All he could think about was how mad his mom would be and then to top things off his teacher is going to call....

He shook his head, groaning. "I'll be on punishment forever."

Half way home, the rain started falling, causing Lee to pick up his pace. His quick steps turned into running.

He reached the end of the street and halted. With no traffic light and the crossing guard gone, he was on his own. Following his parents' instructions, he looked to the left and to the right, waiting for the speeding traffic to slow down.

Fidgeting, Lee waited for a chance to cross the street. A man in a white car drove up to the sidewalk curb, stopped and leaned out the window.

"Hi, Lee, do you want a ride?"

He ignored the man and concentrated on the fast moving traffic. Waiting to cross the busy intersection, Lee watched the man park his car and climb out.

The man walked toward him and stopped. "Lee, let me give you a ride home."

All he could hear was his mother's voice. "Do not talk to strangers."

"Lee, did you hear me? You're getting wet."

Again, Lee heard his mother's warning. "Don't talk to strangers."

"Don't you remember me?"

Lee gazed up at the towering, heavy set man and cocked his head to the side. The stranger seemed familiar but…. He wasn't sure.

Reaching for Lee's hand, the man said, "If nothing else let me help you cross the street."

Lee shook his head.

"Okay, but it's raining hard and you're getting soak. I bet your mother would want me to give you a ride home.

Lee thought, *"How did the man know his mother?"* While he was thinking, the man grabbed his hand.

"Come on Lee."

Struggling, Lee tried to free his hand from the man's strong grip. He opened his mouth to yell for help, but changed his mind. He relaxed and smiled. This man wasn't a stranger.

Lee grinned. "I remember you now. My mother gave you permission to buy me a candy bar."

"That's right. Now, can I give you a ride home?"

Lee nodded his head.

Once inside the car, the man handed him a candy bar.

"Thank you."

Lee removed the candy bar wrapper and glanced up. He yelled, "Stop! You're going the wrong way." He pointed. "You're supposed to make a right turn on Fourth Street."

The man didn't acknowledge Lee. Instead, he kept driving in the wrong direction.

"Stop the car!"

Lee pulled on the door handle and pushed the button to lower the car window, but it wouldn't go down. He banged on the window and screamed, but no one could hear him.

The man continued driving, ignoring Lee's cries and attempts of getting out of the car.

THE CANDY MAN
DISCUSSION QUESTIONS

A conversation may generate from the story. If it does not, the questions below are offered as a starting point for a discussion.

1. What could Lee have done when the man asked him if he wanted a ride?

2. Explain why the man was or was not a stranger to Lee.

3. What could Lee have done once he was in the car?

2

THE EMERGENCY

Robin Baker glanced up at the wall clock in her office. Frustrated and angry, she yelled, "I can't believe it. I'm late again picking Roger up from school."

With one quick motion, she cleaned off the top of her desk. Grabbing her briefcase, she rushed toward the door. The phone rang when she placed her hand on the doorknob.

Against her better judgment, she answered it. "Hello."

"Hello, is this Mrs. Baker?"

"Yes, it is." Robin did not recognize the deep baritone voice, but it sounded familiar.

"How can I help you?"

"I'm Officer Franklin." The man paused. "I'm calling about your son. He's...."

Robin interrupted the man, her voice full of concern. "What's wrong? Is Roger okay?"

"Ma'am, Roger's fine, but he's being taken to Memorial Hospital."

"What happened?"

"There's been an accident. You're needed at the hospital."

"Wait…." The phone went dead before Robin had a chance to ask any questions or obtain any information.

Hanging up the phone, Robin sprinted out of the office. Inside her car, she pulled her cell phone out of her purse and dialed her husband, Kevin's telephone number.

Kevin picked up the file folder off his desk. Heading off to his meeting, the intercom buzzed.

"Yes, Margo."

"Your wife is on line one." The secretary added, "She says it's an emergency."

"Thank you."

"Hi, Robin, what's up? I don't have much time. I'm on my way to a meeting."

Robin's words were mixed with sobs, making it difficult for Kevin to understand what she was saying. "Slow down, Honey and tell me what's wrong."

Clearing her throat, Robin tried again. "I received a telephone call from the police department." Sniveling, she mumbled. "Roger's been in an accident and he was taken to Memorial Hospital."

Kevin's grip on the phone tightened. He spoke with a comforting tone, hoping to sound composed. "Honey, calm down and tell me what else the officer said."

She let out a loud cry. "That's all he said."

"It's okay, honey." His voice cracked. "Everything's going to be okay. Where are you now?"

"I'm on my way to the hospital."

"I'll meet you there in twenty minutes."

Every time a car passed by, Roger grew more anxious. He cringed watching the last bus drive off. He walked up and down the sidewalk, wishing his mother wasn't always late picking him up after school. On his next birthday, he would turn ten years old and instead of his mother picking him up, he could ride the school bus home.

He stopped pacing and sat down on the school concrete steps. He pulled his math book out of his backpack. Before opening it, he spotted a man walking toward him.

The man stopped and with a wide grin said, "Hi. Are you Roger Baker?"

Roger stared at the man, but did not answer. His mother's warning words echoed in his head. "Don't talk to strangers."

"Aren't you Roger Baker?"

Roger wondered how the man knew his name. After several minutes of silence, he answered. "Yes, but...."

"I know. You're not supposed to talk to strangers. I'm Officer Franklin. Don't worry, your mom told me your name. She asked me to pick you up."

"Why?"

"There's been an accident."

Roger's eyes widened. He jumped up and the book fell on the step. "Is my mom okay?"

The man touched Roger's shoulder, staring into his eyes. "It's okay, son. Your mom's fine. Your dad was the one in the accident."

Roger shook his head. "I don't believe you."

"I'm telling you the truth, son."

With confidence, Roger gave the man a defiant glare. "If my dad was in an accident, my mom would have picked me up."

The man nodded. "You're right, but your mom is at the hospital and that's why she sent me."

"Okay, but all the policemen I know wear uniforms."

The man chuckled. "You're a smart boy, Roger. Most police officers do wear uniforms, but not all of them."

Roger's eyes narrowed. "Okay, then show me your badge."

The man pulled a wallet from his coat pocket, opened it and showed Roger his badge.

The man closed his wallet and put it away. "Do you believe me now?"

Roger shrugged.

The man urged. "We need to hurry."

Roger picked up his book and put it inside his backpack. He followed the man down the steps.

THE EMERGENCY

DISCUSSION QUESTIONS

A conversation may generate from the story. If it does not, the questions below are offered as a starting point for a discussion.

1. What else could Roger do when he questioned the police officer's identity?

2. What other choices did Roger have besides going with the police officer?

3. What types of emergency plans have your families made in such situations?

3

THE BALLON

In the fall, Lorrie Haley and her two best girlfriends, Traci Webster and Denise Browne, were entering the fifth grade. They chatted with excitement.

They all agreed that this was the best summer. Their parents had given them permission to attend the annual back-to-school festival without having parental supervision or a sister or brother tagging along.

The girls gathered at Lorrie's house. She lived about one block from the park where the event was being held. They decided to dress alike, white shorts and pink tank tops.

Before the girls left for the park, Lorrie's mother gave them two instructions. "At all times, I want you girls to stay together and every hour check-in at the large white pavilion. Either I or one of your parents will meet you there. Do you understand?"

"Yes ma'am." They said in unison.

"The first check-in is at one o'clock." She added, "Who's wearing a watch?"

Lorrie raised her arm and pointed to her wrist.

"Okay, girls have a good time, and I'll see you in an hour."

When the girls arrived at the park, they strolled around, surveying all the activities.

Wide-eyed, Traci exclaimed, "The festival is bigger than last year."

Lorrie exclaimed. "Can you believe that the hottest teen band in the county is the main feature?"

Denise added, "Yeah and did you see all the different food vendors and games to play?"

Before they decided what they wanted to do, it was one o'clock, time to check-in. They rushed over to the pavilion and talked to Lorrie's mom.

"Thanks girls for being on time. Traci's mom will see you at two."

The girls strolled off and stopped at a food vendor. After buying hot dogs, fries, and sodas, they found an empty park bench and sat down.

While eating, they watched a clown giving away balloons. He made his way towards their table.

Denise whispered. "I hope he doesn't come over to us because we're too old for balloons?"

The clown did stop and asked, "Which one of you pretty girls have a dog?"

Denise raised her hand. "I have a poodle."

The clown blew up about ten balloons. He moved his fingers at a quick pace, twisting and turning them into different shapes. Finished, he handed Denise a balloon that resembled a poodle.

The girls clapped their hands, showing their appreciation.

The clown turned to Traci. "What's your favorite animal?"

"I like elephants."

Again, the clown did his magic, and handed Traci the finished creation. She gushed, "It really looks like an elephant."

Traci and Denise beamed showing their balloon-like animals to the girls and boys who had gathered around them.

Lorrie wanted one, but the clown turned around and was walking away. She ran after him.

"Excuse me. Would you make me a balloon animal?"

The clown patted his pockets. "I'm sorry. I don't have any more balloons." He paused. "I have more in my van. If you follow me, I'll make whatever you want."

He pointed. "My van's over there."

Lorrie chewed on her lower lip. She thought about her mother's instructions. "Stay together."

"Traci. Denise." She yelled. They didn't answer her. She tried again. "Traci. Denise."

The clown shrugged and started walking away from her.

One more time, she tried getting her friends' attention. Again, they didn't respond. She ran after the clown thinking, *"I'll only be gone for a few minutes."*

Lorrie and the clown reached the van and he said, "Since you came with me, look what I have just for you." He opened the van doors.

She gasped. Her eyes twinkled seeing all the toys and stuffed animals.

The clown held out his hand. "Let me help you get inside."

Lorrie hesitated. "I don't know."

He glanced down at Lorrie and whispered. "I have a secret, but you have to promise not to tell anyone." Before Lorrie answered, he rushed on. "I'm Mr. Shane from church."

Lorrie wasn't convinced. Her eyes narrowed, inspecting him. "I don't believe you."

"It's really me." He went into his pocket and pulled out a wallet. He showed her his driver's license.

She glanced at it and squealed. "Mr. Shane, it is you."

"Come on. Let me help you get inside." He took her hand, and she climbed in.

"You can pick out whatever you want."

Lorrie picked up several stuffed animals, but put them down. Her eyes spotted a big, brown teddy bear. She hugged it and smiled. *"Wait until Traci and Denise see what I have. It's better than some dumb old animal made from a balloon."*

When she turned around to climb out of the van, Mr. Shane closed the doors.

###

Traci and Denise stood up. It was time to meet Traci's mom at the pavilion.

"Where's Lorrie?" Denise glanced around.

"She was sitting right here. Where did she go?" Traci shrugged. "I don't know, but it's two o'clock. We don't have time to look for her. Maybe she's already...."

Denise shook her head. "She wouldn't leave without telling us where she was going."

Irritated, Traci said, "Well, she's not here, and we need to go."

"Wait. Let's ask some of our friends if they saw her leave." They asked, but no one remembered seeing her.

Traci insisted. "Denise, we need to go."

When they reached the pavilion, Lorrie wasn't there.

THE BALLOON
DISCUSSION QUESTIONS

A conversation may generate from the story. If it does not, the questions below are offered as a starting point for a discussion.

1. What should Lorrie have done about getting a balloon?

2. How should Lorrie have dealt with her friends when she tried to get their attention?

3. What else could Lorrie have done other than follow the clown to his van?

4

TOP DOLLAR STORE

Every Saturday, Auntie picked up her three nieces and two nephews. Their ages ranged from four to ten.

She enjoyed taking them to the Top Dollar Store where everything cost one dollar. She didn't have any children of her own and loved spending time with them. She believed their weekly trip to the store helped to teach them independence and lessons about money.

Arriving at Top Dollar, Auntie parked the car and made her usual speech. "Before we go inside, remember the rules. Number one, there will be no running. Number two, you have three dollars to spend or to keep. Number three, since Rosie is the oldest, Joey and Stevie you'll go with her. Lastly, I'll be in my usual spot, upfront, sitting in one of the chairs, waiting for you."

Auntie finished and they piled out of the car. They walked single file inside to the store.

The two girls scurried off in a different direction than Rosie, Joey and Stevie. Rosie stood in the middle of the two boys, grabbing their hands before they had a chance to run off.

Walking down the main aisle, Joey yanked on Rosie's arm, pulling her towards an aisle to the right. He was strong, making it difficult for her to hold onto his hand.

In a firm voice, she said, "Stop it, Joey! If you want to look at something, ask me."

Jumping up and down, he pointed. "I want to look at the trucks, over there."

They walked over to the toys. After picking up several trucks, Joey held up a blue one. "I want to buy this one."

"Okay." Rosie turned her attention to Stevie. "Do you see anything you want to buy?"

"No, I need to pee." He crossed his legs and with urgency said, "I need to go now."

Pursing her lips tight and leaning close to him, Rosie asked, "Didn't Auntie tell you to use the bathroom before we left the house?"

Tears brimmed Stevie's eyes. "Yes, but...." He whimpered, "I didn't need to go then, but I have to go now."

Picking him up, Rosie said, "Joey, stay close to me." They hurried to the restroom, located at the back of the store near the loading dock.

Using her back, Rosie pushed on the restroom's door. Before she went it, Joey sat down on the floor. He had turned his attention to playing with the toy truck.

With determination, he said, "I'll stay here and play with my truck. I don't need to pee."

Stevie squirmed, pleading, "I need to pee."

"Joey, get up." He didn't budge.

Rosie warned. "Get up. You have to go inside with us." She reached for his hand, but he dodged her attempt to grab him.

Joey was adamant. "I'm a big boy. I can wait right here."

Stevie yelled, "I need to pee."

Rather than argue with Joey and perhaps make Stevie wet his pants, Rosie glared at him and warned. "You better not move! We'll be right back."

Stevie finished and Rosie held him up to the sink. "Wash your hands, so we can go."

Rosie opened the door, but Joey wasn't on the floor where she had left him. She grabbed Stevie's hand and hurried down the first aisle, near the restroom and yelled, "Joey, Joey." She rushed down another aisle, calling his name.

Spotting her sisters, Rosie approached them, hoping her voice was calm. "Have you seen Joey?"

In unison they said, "No. Why?"

Rather than answer them, she turned and continued her search. With no luck, she dashed to the front of the store.

Hearing Rosie call Joey's name, Auntie stood up, watching Rosie rushing toward her. "What's wrong?"

Sobbing, Rosie murmured, "I took Stevie to the restroom. I left Joey outside the door, playing with a truck. When I returned, Joey wasn't there. I've searched the store and I can't find him."

TOP DOLLAR STORE DISCUSSION QUESTIONS

A conversation may generate from the story. If it does not, the questions below are offered as a starting point for a discussion.

1. What should Auntie have done when taking her nieces and nephews to the Top Dollar Store every Saturday?

2. What instructions should Auntie have given the children about using the restroom?

3. What could Rosie have done when her brother, Joey refused to go inside the restroom?

5
UNCLE BOBBY

Nine-year old Jodi didn't understand the relationship between her dad and his best friend, Bobby Ludwich. Ever since she could remember her parents instructed her to call him, "Uncle Bobby."

Since he wasn't her dad's brother, she didn't know why she had to call him, Uncle Bobby. Her dad explained it when she asked.

"Bobby has been my best friend since elementary school. He's like my brother. The reason I want you to call him Uncle Bobby is because he doesn't have sisters, brothers, wife, children, nieces or nephews."

Jodi understood her dad's explanation, but it didn't make a difference to her. With every birthday, she became more uncomfortable being around Uncle Bobby. She didn't know how to explain it to her parents.

###

Jodi was helping her mother fix dinner when she said, "Uncle Bobby is coming to dinner, tonight."

"Can I have dinner in my room?"

"Why?" Her mother asked.

"I…I don't want to see Uncle Bobby."

Her dad arrived home from work when he heard what Jodi said. "How are my favorite girls?" He kissed the top of Jodi's head and then walked over to his wife and gave her a kiss.

"What were you saying about Uncle Bobby when I walked into the kitchen?"

She shrugged. "I don't want to see him."

Puzzled, her mother asked, "Honey, did Uncle Bobby do something to you?"

Jodi shook her head.

"Then what's wrong?" Her dad wanted an explanation.

"Dad, I know Bob…Uncle Bobby is your friend, but he gives me the creeps."

"When did he start giving you the creeps?"

"I don't know. I guess it's when he hugs me."

Her mother defended Uncle Bobby. "Honey, he hugs everyone. That's his way of saying he likes you."

"Okay, but does he have to kiss me?" Jodi paused and crinkled her nose. "His kisses are wet and gooey."

· "I know what you mean." Her mother laughed and stuck her tongue out. "Ugh...his kisses are sloppy."

"Well, does he have to kiss me?"

Her dad's voice was gruff. "Listen young lady. Bobby is like family and our friend. He has no one else. It's not like you see him every day. It won't hurt you to be nice to him. Do you understand?"

She didn't answer.

Her dad's voice was stern. "Young lady, do you understand?"

She shrugged.

Her mother agreed with her dad. "Uncle Bobby loves you and would never harm you. It won't hurt you to show him some kindness."

"Jodi, I'm warning you." Her dad's voice was firm. "Don't say or do anything to hurt Bobby's feelings."

"You and mom don't understand. I just don't want him to touch me."

"Well, your mother and I don't understand. Right now, I don't want to hear any more about this. Do you understand?" When Jodi didn't answer, her dad asked again, "Do you understand?"

"Yes, sir."

Lorraine M. Harris

UNCLE BOBBY
DISCUSSION QUESTIONS

A conversation may generate from the story. If it does not, the questions below are offered as a starting point for a discussion.

1. What should Jodi's parents have done about her concerns?

2. Should Jodi's parents talk to Uncle Bobby? If yes or no, explain your answer.

3. Why do you think Jodi's parents don't want to believe what Jodi is implying about Uncle Bobby?

6

SMILE

By some parents' standards, Linda Thomason was too protective. She loved her only child, Maggie, and wanted to keep her safe. Recently, the talk shows had focused on people abducting boys and girls of all ages. It was her job to make sure it did not happen to her daughter.

Linda was upset and worried because she could not be a chaperone for Maggie's class field trip. They were going to the petting zoo.

Before Maggie left for school, Linda reminded her of the *"rules,"* emphasizing each point.

"Remember, no talking to strangers. Do not go with a stranger, even to help find a lost puppy or cat. Do not get into a stranger's car. Yell if someone tries to take you against your will. Last, make sure you can see the teacher or chaperone at all times." Linda paused and looked at her daughter. "Do you understand?"

"Yes, Momma," Maggie replied. She wanted to say but did not, "Mom, I know the rules backwards and forwards. You remind me every time I leave the house."

Before Maggie's class departed for the petting zoo, the teacher divided the boys and girls into three groups of ten. Maggie was happy being in her best friend, Carrie Taylor's group. In addition, Carrie's mother was their group's chaperone.

They arrived at the zoo. After everyone was off the bus, Mrs. Taylor gathered everyone in a circle. Maggie rolled her eyes. She knew what was coming.

Having everyone's attention, Mrs. Taylor began. "I want everyone to stay together. Do not wander off. If you need to use the restroom, let me know. No one will go anywhere by themselves. I want everyone to take a partner. Does everyone understand?"

In unison, the children responded. "Yes, Mrs. Taylor."

The group's first stop was the tortoise area. The children's eyes widened watching the large animal move in slow motion. The boys and girls touched and rubbed the tortoise's hard shell and he didn't seem to mind.

The potbelly pig pen was the next stop. A woman stood with a camera, taking pictures of the pigs. Seeing the children, she turned and stopped three of the girls and aimed the camera. "Smile. Smile."

The woman was about to snap another picture when Mrs. Taylor rushed over to the girls and stood in front of them.

"Excuse me, what do you think you're doing?"

The woman lowered the camera. "I'm sorry. I should have asked permission before taking the girls' picture."

She flashed a badge that hung around her neck. "I work for the local newspaper. I'm writing an article about the petting zoo."

Mrs. Taylor uttered, "Oh…I see."

The woman paused and cocked her head to the side. "Is it okay if I take a few pictures of the girls and boys? The pictures would add to the article."

Mrs. Taylor shook her head. "I don't know."

"I'll tell you what, why don't you pose with the children?"

Mrs. Taylor touched her hair. "Oh….no….no…I couldn't. My hair is a mess." She chewed on her lower lip. "I guess there's no harm in you taking the children's picture."

When the woman finished taking the pictures, she walked over to Mrs. Taylor and smiled.

"Thank you. I really appreciate you letting me take the pictures. I understand your initial reaction. You can't be too careful."

"I agree. Well, we really have to go."

"Oh, before I forget, can you give me the names and addresses of the children?"

Mrs. Taylor was confused. "Why would I give you that information?"

"I need them for the newspaper article. Their names will appear under the picture."

Mrs. Taylor blushed. "Of course, what was I thinking about?" She opened her purse and pulled out a folded paper. She handed it to the woman.

The woman began walking away, turned and said, "Thanks again." She paused. "Since I have each child's address, I'll send them a picture."

SMILE
DISCUSSION QUESTIONS

A conversation may generate from the story. If it does not, the questions below are offered as a starting point for a discussion.

1. Besides the badge, what identification should Mrs. Taylor have requested from the woman who wanted to take pictures?

2. Why do you think Mrs. Taylor gave the woman permission to take pictures of the children?

3. Explain why or why not Mrs. Taylor should give the woman the names and addresses of the children.

7

LET NO ONE IN

Ten-year old Troy Greene arrived home from school, changed clothes and sat at the kitchen table to do his homework. The doorbell rang and he peeked out the front window. A van marked Sunlight Cable was in the driveway. A man stood on the porch, dressed in a uniform.

Again, the doorbell rang. Troy opened the front door and talked through the locked glass storm door. "May I help you?"

"Yes. Some of the neighbors called and said the cable service is out. I'm going door-to-door checking out the problem."

Troy's homework was not done and he had not turned on the TV. He didn't know if the cable was working. Not knowing what to do, he shut the door and called his mother on her cell phone.

"Hi, Troy. What's up?"

"A man from the cable company is at the door. He said there is a problem with the cable service in the neighborhood. He wants to check ours."

"Ask the man to show you a work ID."

Troy did what his mother said. He turned his back to the man and whispered, "Mom, he showed me an ID. What do you want me to do?"

"Let him in. I'll be home in less than fifteen minutes."

Judy pulled into the driveway, but there was no cable truck in the driveway. She climbed out of the car and walked up the sidewalk. She unlocked the front door and yelled, "Troy, I'm home."

She shut the door and called out again. No answer. She walked from room to room, trying to find her son. She fumed. "Where are you Troy?"

She went out into the back yard, but he wasn't there either. She called his best friend, Carl. Waiting for someone to answer her call, she ticked off the rules she had given Troy.

"Don't let anyone in the house including your friends. Eat only the snacks left in the refrigerator. Complete your homework before watching TV or playing video games. No talking on the phone to your friends and do not go to their house." Why had he disobeyed her?

Carl answered the phone and said he had not seen Troy since they were on the school bus. He gave her the number of several other boys who might have seen him. She called them, but they repeated what Carl said.

Next, she called her neighbor and friend, Ruthie Nelson. She lived down the street. "Hi Ruthie, can I come over?"

"Sure, but what's wrong?

"I'll tell you what's going on when I get there."

Hurrying down the street, Judy thought about the past six months. Nothing prepared her for her husband's massive heart attack and his death.

During the fifteen years of Judy's marriage, she had the luxury of not working outside of the home and raising her son. When her husband died, she went from a stay-at-home mom to a full-time working mom.

Although Judy had not worked in years, she had kept her nursing licenses up-to-date. With a shortage of registered nurses, she had no problem getting hired at the local hospital.

The one problem she encountered entering back into the work force was child care for her son, Troy. Ruthie volunteered to keep him when she worked the night shift.

For weeks she agonized over what she should do with Troy when she worked the day shift. She shared her concerns with Troy.

He argued. "I'm too old for a babysitter and all my friends take care of themselves after school."

School started in less than a week and with no other options, she relented to Troy's suggestion and he became a *"latch key kid."* She hated the idea, but what could she do?

She suppressed her thoughts arriving at Ruthie's house. She rang the doorbell.

Ruthie opened the door and knew from Judy's reddened eyes and tear stained face that something was wrong. "Come in and tell me what's going on."

"Troy's not at home."

She threw her hands up in the air and through sobs fumed. "This is why I didn't want him having the responsibility of staying at home alone after school."

"Don't blame yourself. You had no choice, but to work."

"You're right, but…." Judy's voice cracked. "Maybe I should have taken a job that didn't require me to work day and night shifts."

Ruthie didn't respond to her statement. "Have you called his friends?"

"Yes and the last time they saw him was on the school bus." She ran her hand through her hair. "When you arrived home from work, did you see him?"

"No, but let me think." Ruthie closed her eyes. She opened them and exclaimed.

"The only thing I remember was the Sunlight Cable Company van parked in your driveway."

"Troy called me about that. Something happened with the cable service and I told him to let the…." Not finishing her sentence, she screamed.

"Oh my God, what have I done? I told Troy to let the man in. He had an employee ID and…."

Ruthie put her arms around Judy. "It's okay." She eased her embrace. "I'll call the police."

Two police officers arrived and Judy told them about Troy being missing and the cable man.

The officers listened. After which, one asked, "How old is your son?"

"He's ten."

Judy picked up a picture Ruthie had on the nearby table. She handed it to the police officer and whispered. "He lets himself in after school until I come home from work."

Through tears she asked, "What's going to happen?"

"One more question, Ma'am. Could your son have run away?"

"No…no way." Judy shook her head.

She murmured. "I know something happened to him."

"Please find him," she pleaded.

The police officer explained. "I'm going to send his picture to my Captain who will make arrangements for an Amber Alert. The radio and TV stations will make the announcement about your missing son. After that, we'll have to wait and hope someone calls with information about him."

Lorraine M. Harris

LET NO ONE IN
DISCUSSION QUESTIONS

A conversation may generate from the story. If it does not, the questions below are offered as a starting point for a discussion.

1. What does "let <u>no one</u> in" mean?

2. When children are left home alone after school or other times, what should they know about letting people in to perform services such as a cable man, delivery person, etc.?

3. What could the mother have done when her son called about the cable man?

8

THE RESTROOM

A divorced parent, Tom Lester spent every weekend with his two children, Tom Junior, nicknamed, TJ, and Teresa. During their visits, he planned an activity for them. On Saturday, they were going to the movies at the shopping mall.

In unison, excited, they said, "We want to see a Disney movie."

"Okay, but remember, no popcorn, candy, or drinks. We'll buy something to eat and drink after the movie." He paused. "Is that okay?"

They smiled, bobbing their heads up and down.

The movie ended and at the mall's food court, TJ asked, "Can we have Chinese food?"

"What about you Teresa?"

"Can we use chopsticks?"

"You sure can." They ordered shrimp fried rice and lemonade. For dessert, he treated the children to an ice cream cone.

Finished, Tom stood up. "Okay kids, it's time to leave."

"Daddy, I need to use the bathroom." Teresa said.

Tom frowned. This was the first time he had been faced with this problem. He didn't want to take his daughter into the men's restroom and he couldn't go into the ladies' restroom.

He peered down at his daughter. "Can you wait until we get home?"

She shook her head. "No. I need to go now."

TJ whined, "I need to go too."

Tom ran his hand through his hair. He didn't know what to do. Now both children had to use the bathroom. He glanced around. Holding his children's hands, he walked over to the information desk.

"Miss, could you tell me where the restrooms are?"

The woman pointed. "Yes, they're located down the corridor, near the back mall exit."

"Thank you."

Teresa crossed her legs, tugging on her dad's sleeve. She whispered. "I really need to pee."

Her dad grabbed his children's hands and dashed down the hallway. Tom remembered that most malls had family restrooms. He frowned. This one didn't.

Teresa shook her right leg. "Daddy, I need to go, now."

"Wait a minute."

A woman was about to go into the ladies restroom. He stopped her.

"Can I ask you to take my daughter inside the Ladies' Restroom? I can't take her inside the Men's Restroom with me and I don't want her going inside alone."

"Sure, I'll do it." The woman grabbed Teresa's hand and went inside.

Tom and TJ finished and stood outside the Ladies' Restroom door, waiting for Teresa. They watched a number of women and children going in and coming out of the ladies' room, but no Teresa. Tom grew anxious.

Before the next woman went inside the restroom, Tom stopped her. "Miss, my daughter's inside there. Will you check to see if she's okay? Her name is Teresa."

The woman agreed. She returned, confused. "Are you sure your daughter is inside the ladies' room?"

"Yes. Why?"

"I checked every stall and no one is inside there. I'm sorry."

Tom took out his cell phone and call 911.

THE RESTROOM
DISCUSSION QUESTIONS

A conversation may generate from the story. If it does not, the questions below are offered as a starting point for a discussion.

1. What could Teresa's father have done so she didn't have to go into the restroom by herself?

2. Why did Teresa's father agree to let the woman take her into the restroom?

3. What else could Teresa's father have done besides allowing her to go into the restroom with the strange woman?

Lorraine M. Harris

SIXTH GRADE AND OLDER

9

PHOTO SHOOT

Julie Carter gave birth to a beautiful daughter with auburn hair and green eyes. She named her Star. Julie believed her baby was destined for stardom.

At sixteen, Star had a model-like figure, tall and slender. Julie's prediction about Star's fame came sooner than she expected.

After a school play, a woman approached Julie. "Hello. My name is Mrs. Jean Miller. I'm a fashion coordinator at the Stone Department Store. I think your daughter would make a beautiful model. Would she be interested in a modeling job?"

Julie didn't think twice about accepting the offer for Star. She wanted nothing but success for Star and would do everything to make it happen.

###

It was the first of the month and Julie had to make some decisions about what bills to pay. She went through the stack, giving each one consideration. The slam of the front door made her glance up.

"Mom, Mom."

"What's wrong?"

Star's face beamed like sunshine. "You're not going to believe this. Teen Model Magazine selected three girls for the fall issue." She exclaimed. "And I'm one of them."

Her mother hugged her. "Congratulations. Honey, this is a lifetime opportunity. You're on your way." She eased her embrace. "Let's celebrate. How about if we go to Mickey D's and get a salad?"

"Okay. But, mom before you get too excited, there is one catch.

"What is it?"

"In two weeks, I need a portfolio with professional photos."

Worried lines formed on Julie's forehead. She was a single parent, working a full-time and part-time job that didn't pay all the bills. How could she get the money for the photos?"

Star watched her mom's pained expression. Times like this is when Star wished the department store paid her rather than giving her store credit to buy clothes.

"Mom, I have an idea. Why don't I use the babysitting money I've been saving to pay for the photos?"

Julie gathered her daughter into her arms. She didn't want Star to see the tears that threatened to fall.

"You're so thoughtful, but you've been saving that money to buy a car."

She let go of Star and smiled. "Don't worry. I'll find a way to get the money."

Star bit her lower lip and whispered. "Mom, it's no big deal. There will be other opportunities."

"Are you kidding?" Julie shook her head. "Opportunities like this don't come that often. I'll think of something."

After school, Star went to the department store before going home. She had to talk to Mrs. Miller. She was like a grandmother to the teen models and they had nicknamed her Granny M.

Star walked into the office where Mrs. Wright, the secretary greeted her.

"Hi, Star."

"Hello, Mrs. Wright. Is Granny M in?" She hurried on. "She's not expecting me, but it's kind of important."

"Let me check." Mrs. Wright picked up the phone. "Star Carter is here and wants to see you."

"Star, you can go in."

"Thanks Mrs. Wright."

Star entered the office and Granny M glanced up from the paper she was holding. "Hi, Star. What a pleasant surprise. Have a seat." Star sat in the chair in front of Granny M's desk.

"What brings you here today?"

Star cleared her throat. "I need to…." Loud sobs replaced her words.

Granny M stood up and rushed to her. She put her arm around Star's shoulders. "There, there. It's okay. Whatever it is, it can't be that bad." She handed Star a tissue.

She blew her nose.

"Now, tell Granny what's wrong."

Star looked down, twisting the tissue in her hands. "My mom was so excited when I told her about Teen Model Magazine, but… I can't accept the offer."

"Why? What's wrong?"

"I…." Star lowered her head and murmured. "I…we don't have the money for the professional photo shoot."

"I see." Granny M patted Star's hand. "I shouldn't tell you this, but you're not the only one, needing money for the photos."

Surprised, Star's head jerked up. "I'm not."

"No, you're not. One of the other girls came to me with the same problem."

"So, what's going to happen?" Star asked.

"Well, there's this modeling job that needed two girls. One job was filled, but there's still one opening. Do you think you'd want the job?"

Eager, Star said, "Yes, yes I want the job. When can I start?"

"Well…." Granny M paused and glanced at her watch. "What about now?"

"Uh….I don't' know. I should discuss this with my mom."

She shrugged. "Okay, but I thought you needed the money."

"I do, but…." Star chewed on her fingernail glancing at the wall clock.

"Can I use your phone? I want to call mom?"

"Of course dear, go ahead."

Star hung up the phone. "I couldn't reach her, but I left a message. I don't know what to do."

"I know your mom." She smiled. "She would say, take the job."

"You really think so?"

"Yes, I do. She wants the best for you and wants to see you succeed." Granny M paused. "You don't want to disappoint her. So, will you let me make the arrangements?"

Although Star trusted Granny M, she wasn't sure what to do. She glanced up and Granny M was waiting for her answer. At last Star responded. "Okay, make the arrangements."

Granny M made a telephone call. After writing something on a piece of paper, she handed it to Star.

"Everything's been arranged. I wrote down the address where you're going." She reached inside her purse and handed Star a ten dollar bill. "This is for the taxi fare."

Star's eyes widened, her voice quivering. "You're not coming with me?"

Shaking her head, Granny M explained. "I have several other appointments and I can't leave the office for at least another hour."

"Uh... I don't know. I don't feel comfortable going alone."

"Star, do you trust me?"

She nodded.

"I would never put you in a situation to harm you. There's no reason to worry. Mr. Kilmer is expecting you. Now, hurry along."

Star gazed out the window while the taxi maneuvered through traffic. She became apprehensive when the driver made a turn onto an isolated street. Some of the buildings had boarded windows, making them seem vacant. The taxi slowed and parked outside a large, gray brick building.

Star made no attempt to climb out of the taxi.

"Miss, this is the address." The man turned around. "Is everything okay?"

"Uh...yes." She paid the driver and climbed out.

Star entered the unmarked building. In the foyer, a door on the left had the word, *studio*, written on it. She opened the door and walked down a long narrow corridor. The dense carpeting muffled the sound of her shoes.

At the end of the hallway she reached another door. She opened it and went in. The room's lighting was dim. Star squinted, trying to adjust her eyes. The tall dark shadows made the hairs stand up on the back of her neck.

Rapid heart-beats pounded against her chest. "Hello. Is anyone here?"

From behind her a deep baritone voice made Star jump and turn around.

"I didn't mean to startle you. You must be Star." The man extended his hand. "I've been waiting for you. I'm Mr. Kilmer. Please follow me."

Star trailed behind him. When they walked into another room, she surveyed the contents. The room contained a sofa, chair, bed, and a camera on a tripod. She felt uneasy.

"Mr…Mr. Kilmer."

He turned around. "Is something wrong?"

"I've…I've changed my mind and…."

A sharp object pinched Star's arm. Her vision went blurry, her head began spinning and then everything went black.

PHOTO SHOOT
DISCUSSION QUESTIONS

A conversation may generate from the story. If it does not, the questions below are offered as a starting point for a discussion.

1. Explain whether you believe Star is modeling more for herself or for her mother.

2. What type of conversations should Star's mother have had with her regarding her budding modeling career?

3. When Star couldn't reach her mother, what should she have done about the modeling job Granny M offered her?

10

THE NEIGHBOR

Fourteen-year-old Chucky wanted a summer job, but couldn't find one. His mom suggested he ask some of the neighbors if he could cut their grass or run errands for them.

He was hired by several people. His favorite person whom he worked for was Mrs. Jones. He called her Mrs. J. She reminded him of his first-grade teacher. She had the prettiest dark brown hair with matching eyes. Her smile was like sunshine, bright and cheery. Chucky liked Mrs. J and from her hugs and the kisses she planted on his cheeks, he knew she had similar feelings.

When school started, he thrilled at the number of neighbors who retained his services. He beamed when Mrs. J was one of them.

The new work arrangement posed one problem. He no longer saw Mrs. J every week. He missed their visits and talks.

Sometimes he walked home from school instead of taking the bus. In doing so, he passed Mrs. J's house, in hopes of seeing her. Today, he was in luck. Turning the corner, he spotted her, carrying a large package.

He ran and caught up with her. Out of breath, he spoke. "Hi, Mrs. J."

"Hi, Chucky. What a pleasant surprise to see you. How was school today?"

He shrugged. "I guess it was okay." He insisted. "Please let me carry your package?"

"Thank you. You're always so thoughtful."

They talked and laughed while discussing last night's baseball game. Unlike most girls, she liked sports.

The walk ended too soon. Standing at the end of her sidewalk, she asked, "Why don't you come in?"

Chucky thought about her invitation. He wasn't supposed to go inside of anyone's house without his parents' permission. *But, what was the big deal?*

Mrs. J watched Chucky, waiting for an answer. "Come on." She urged. "I want to show you my baseball collection."

His eyes grew wide. "I would love to see it, but...."

"I'll tell you what. Come inside and I'll call your mother and let her know where you are."

Chucky smiled and thought, *"What a great idea! He could kiss Mrs. J for suggesting that she call his mother. This way, he wouldn't have to listen to his mom yelling at him for disobeying the rules."*

She unlocked the front door, walked inside and held it open. "Are you coming in?"

He entered. She closed and locked the door behind them.

"Have a seat. Would you like a soda?"

"Sure, that's fine."

Mrs. J went to the kitchen and returned, carrying two glasses. While handing Chucky his drink, she said, "I called your mom."

He smiled and began drinking his soda. Mrs. J watched him drain it empty.

Chucky put the glass on the coffee table and leaned back against the sofa's cushions. His head began swirling. He tried sitting up, but fell backwards. The room was blurry. His head felt woozy and then everything went black.

THE NEIGHBOR
DISCUSSION QUESTIONS

A conversation may generate from the story. If it does not, the questions below are offered as a starting point for a discussion.

1. Why do you think Chucky disobeyed his parents' rule of not going inside someone's house without their permission?

2. What should Chucky have done when Mrs. J invited him in?

3. Explain whether you believe Chucky should have told his parents about his crush on Mrs. J.

11

BEST FRIENDS

David Locke and Kenny Rosen were best friends. They went to day care together when they were two years old.

They were best friends until they went to middle school. Their friendship began to change. David played sports while Kenny's interest was computers. They continued to hang out together until David made the football team, and he began spending more time with the guys from the football team.

One of David's new-founded friends was Wayne Peters. He was popular and was the quarterback of the football team.

David liked spending time at Wayne's house. He thought Wayne had the coolest dad. He acted more like one of the guys than an adult. He played games with the boys, allowed them to eat plenty of junk food and did not yell at them if they spilled a drink or dropped food on the floor.

The biggest event of the year was Wayne's sleepover party. Every guy in the school wanted an invite. David received his invitation and thought this would be a good time to introduce Kenny to his new friends. He broached the subject to Wayne.

"I don't know, David. I don't even know this guy." Wayne asked, "What did you say his name was?"

"Kenny Rosen."

Wayne cocked his head to the side. "I know most of the football players and…."

"He's not on the team"

"Then why should I invite him"

David told him the truth. "No other reason than he's my best friend."

Wayne shrugged. "Okay, he can come."

David couldn't believe his ears when he discussed the invitation with Kenny. "What do you mean you're not sure you want to come?"

He threw his hands in the air. "Man, there are guys who would do anything to attend this party."

"Let me think about it and I'll get back to you."

Several days later Kenny called David. "I have permission to attend the party, but I'm not sure I'll fit in with these guys."

"Quit worrying. You need to chill a little. Everyone's cool, even Wayne's dad."

Kenny had a backup plan, but he didn't tell David. If for some reason he wasn't having fun, he would call his parents to come and get him.

The day of the sleepover, David's mom drove them to Wayne's house. Mr. Peters answered the door.

"Hey guys. Good to see you, David. Who's your friend?"

David put his arm around Kenny's shoulders. "This is my friend, Kenny."

"Welcome. If you're David's friend, you must be okay. Come on in. The rest of the boys are in the den."

Strolling into the room, David introduced Kenny to everyone. Glancing around, Kenny now understood why everyone wanted to attend the party.

The den was similar to the mall's arcade. It was filled with stand-alone video games and a pool table. To top everything off, in front of the sofa was a large flat screen TV covering almost the entire wall.

Several boys sat on the sofa, playing a video game. They invited him to join them. Later he thought, "David's new friends are pretty cool." He was having more fun than he wanted to admit.

The chatter, laughter and activity stopped when Mr. Peters walked in, holding a tray.

"Is anyone hungry?"

Everyone scrabbled over to him. The boys waited until he arranged the pizza, hot dogs, potato chips, popcorn and canned beer on the table.

Quickly, the boys filled their plates, grabbed a beer and found seats. Kenny watched and remained standing. He didn't take anything to eat or drink.

When Mr. Peters served beer it made Kenny uncomfortable. He knew his parents wouldn't approve.

Mr. Peters eased up to him and put his arm around him. "Is everything okay?" He eyed him. "Don't you want anything to eat or drink?"

After an awkward silence, Kenny shook Mr. Peter's arm off his shoulder. "No thanks. I'm fine."

"I understand." Mr. Peters smirked. "You've never drank beer before." He picked up a can and shoved it towards Kenny. "Just take a sip. You might be surprised and actually like it."

"Thanks, but I don't want any."

"Then, what about a soda?"

"Okay. Do you have ginger ale or something like that?"

"Sure, come with me into the kitchen."

Kenny followed Mr. Peters.

"Have a seat at the table."

Mr. Peters fixed Kenny a drink and handed it to him. He joined him at the table.

Kenny took a big gulp of the clear liquid. He shook his head. He sat the glass down and made a face.

"It tastes funny."

Mr. Peters laughed. "I added a little something to it. It will help you relax a little."

Kenny felt light-headed. His words slurred. "Can I call my parents?" He swallowed. "I don't feel good."

"Sure, but why don't you lay down for a few minutes and then I'll take you home."

Kenny protested. "No, my parents will pick me up." He tried to stand, but he couldn't.

"Here, let me help you."

Mr. Peters put his arm around Kenny's shoulders. He helped him stand up and walked him into a room.

Kenny didn't know what happened, but he freaked, realizing he was in a strange bed, with no clothes on.

BEST FRIENDS
DISCUSSION QUESTIONS

A conversation may generate from the story. If it does not, the questions below are offered as a starting point for a discussion.

1. What should Kenny have done when Mr. Peters offered him a can of beer?

2. What should Kenny have done when Mr. Peters offered him a ride home?

3. Explain why Kenny should or should not have insisted in telling David that he was going home.

12

VARSITY FOOTBALL

Jack Whitman lived with his grandmother. His nickname for her was G-Mom. He was two years old when his mother died from cancer. Within two months, his father died from a drug overdose.

Jack loved his grandmother. He made sure he did nothing to cause her any additional heartache or pain. G-Mom did everything to keep him busy and out of trouble.

Since she loved sports, she enrolled him into all types of organized activities such as football, baseball, basketball and soccer. By age twelve, it was evident that Jack was a natural football player.

He entered high school and tried out for the football team. He could not believe what the coach told him. "As a freshman, you've made the varsity team."

He couldn't wait to share the news with G-Mom. Her reaction wasn't what he expected.

"What's wrong? I thought you would be happy about me making the varsity football team."

She wanted to celebrate, but she knew the reality. Her income came from social security and a part-time job. She knew that playing sports came with a price tag. The school supplied most of the required equipment, but anything else the players would have to buy it.

"I'm happy for you, Baby Boy. I didn't mean to take away your joy. It's...I'm not sure how we'll buy the extra football equipment you might need."

"Don't worry. The money from my part-time job will cover any additional expenses."

G-Mom did not continue the conversation. She knew varsity football would require more of his time than he realized. That might mean he'll have to cut back on his work hours or even worse he may have to quit his part-time job.

G-Mom's concern became an actuality. The required hours Jack had to practice football resulted in fewer work hours and a reduced pay check. In addition, the cost of the additional football equipment was more than they both imagined.

Jack didn't know what to do. He met with the coach and said, "I might have to quit the team."

"Why?"

Jack explained. "I live with my grandmother and she's on a fixed income…."

The coach interrupted him. "Isn't Easy Money your uncle?"

"Yes, but…."

"Hear me out. I grew up with your dad and uncle. I know he'll help you. From time to time, he's helped other football players in the same predicament. Talk to him and tell him I sent you."

This was not what Jack expected from the coach. He wondered what the football players did in exchange for Easy Money's help. With him, everything came with strings attached.

Jack didn't want to get involved with his uncle and his illegal activities. In the neighborhood, everyone suspected him of being the drug dealer and all-around gangster. G-Mom would die if he took money from him.

Jack didn't have to make contact with Easy Money. One day after practice, he was waiting in the school parking lot for him.

Easy Money called out to him. "Hey, Jack."

Jack walked over to his car. "Hey. What's up?"

"That's what I want to know. I hear from coach that you're in need of a few things."

Jack did not respond. He lowered his head.

"Listen, Kid, life is hard and you were given a raw deal losing your mom and dad within several months of each other. I know what your granny thinks of me, but I'm still your blood."

Jack listened, adding nothing to the conversation.

"I know you and your granny are proud people, but this is not the time for pride. I can help."

Jack was about to answer, but Easy Money threw his hand up to silence him. "I'm sure coach told you that I've helped other players. So, what's the problem?" He smirked. "Besides, it doesn't seem right that I'd help everyone, but my own kin."

"What is it going to cost me?"

"Come on Jack. You're my only nephew. I'd do anything for you."

"I'm sure you would, but at what cost?"

Easy Money frowned. "Will you feel better earning the money rather than me giving it to you?"

Jack squared his shoulders and with force said, "That's the only way I'll accept your money." He paused. "In addition, I won't do anything illegal for you."

"I'm insulted." Easy Money covered his heart with his right hand. "Do you believe the coach would jeopardize his football players? The job I have for you is above board. What do you say?"

VARSITY FOOTBALL
DISCUSSION QUESTIONS

A conversation may generate from the story. If it does not, the questions below are offered as a starting point for a discussion.

1. Who could help Jack when or if he needs additional football equipment?

2. What if anything should Jack do about the coach referring him to his uncle for money?

3. Explain why Jack should take money from his uncle rather than work for him.

13

COUSINS

Penny loved and admired her sixteen year old cousin, Angie. They were best friends and had a bond similar to sisters.

Penny noticed that since Angie passed her driving test and received her license, she was moody and upset about something. She called and asked what was going on.

"Dad and mom promised me a car and now they're saying they can't afford it."

"Come on Angie. Times are hard and your dad lost his job."

Tears ran down Angie's face. "I know, but I really wanted a car."

Penny suggested. "Why don't you find a job?"

"Who's going to hire me?"

"Do like lots of other teens and work after school at the fast food restaurants or at the department stores."

"Maybe that's what I'll have to do."

###

Three weeks later, Angie called Penny. "Are we still having our slumber party?"

Excited, Penny shouted. "Yeah."

Penny thought Angie had forgotten about their monthly ritual. They took turns having the slumber party.

"It's my turn to have it. I'll see you on Saturday."

The day of the party, Angie ordered the pizza before Penny arrived. Like always, they took two slices a piece and gave the rest to Angie's sisters and brothers. By sharing the pizza with the little ones, they were guaranteed a little privacy.

They ate, listened to music, danced, and styled each other's hair.

While Angie painted Penny's toenails, she hedged. "How is the job hunting going?"

Angie gushed. "I found a wonderful, paying job and soon I'll be driving my own car."

"What? You've been working and didn't tell me. Give me the details. What type of job is it?"

Angie put the bottle of nail polish down on the nightstand and walked over to the computer. She turned it on and entered her password. Connecting to the Internet, she typed in an address, and a website titled, *Naughty School Girls* appeared on the monitor. Her picture appeared and she clicked on it.

Penny's eyes widened. "I can't believe what I'm seeing." She yelled. "Have you lost your mind?"

"Lower your voice. It's not a big deal. That's why I didn't tell you."

"If your parents find out, they'll kill you."

"They'll never find out. They have no idea how to use the computer and besides it's not a big deal." She paused and added, "All I do is stand in front of the camera and pose. No one knows my name."

"That's not the point. Your picture is out on the Internet."

"So what, I get paid a lot of money for doing nothing. Tony says I'm a natural in front of the camera."

"Who's Tony?"

"He's the man who hired me. He said he can make me a movie star." She chewed on her lower lip. "I'll tell you something if you promise not to tell anyone."

Penny agreed. "Okay, what is it?"

She giggled. "I'm meeting Tony this weekend."

COUSINS
DISCUSSION QUESTIONS

A conversation may generate from the story. If it does not, the questions below are offered as a starting point for a discussion.

1. Explain how Angie has put herself in danger by posing for the Internet website.

2. What should Penny do about what she learned about Angie?

3. Besides Angie's parents, who else could Penny talk to about what Angie's has been doing?

14

SEND ME YOUR PICTURE

Sophomore high school student, Bev Morrison couldn't believe that Harry Chestnut asked her out on a date. He was a senior, popular and the captain of the basketball team.

From Bev's first date, her parents expressed their concerns.

"He's too old for you." Her mother said.

Her father had different apprehensions. "You're too young to have a boyfriend, and he drives." He paused and added, "Besides, I know his type, and he'd better not take advantage of my little girl, or he'll be sorry."

Her mom's advice was, "Don't let him pressure you into doing something you don't want to do."

Although her parents didn't voice it, she knew their concern. They thought Harry might take advantage of her. They had nothing to fear.

They had kissed, but agreed they were too young to have a sexual relationship.

She hoped her parents had been more supportive. It had been difficult hearing negative remarks from them and her peers.

At school, the cheerleaders' comments had been, "She's not pretty, smart, thin or fashionable." The other popular girls asked, "What does he see in her?"

Bev suspected that some of his basketball buddies had made similar statements. While others were asking, "Is she putting out?"

***

Despite what everyone thought Bev and Harry were a couple and enjoyed one other. Her parents took measures to protect her by limiting the time she could spend with him. She could see him on the weekends, but not during the school week.

To stay connected with Harry, Bev sent him email and text messages.

One evening when Bev and Harry were sending messages back and forth, her eyes widened, reading his email.

"What are you wearing?"

Instead of answering him, Bev played coy. "What do you think I'm wearing?"

"I think you're wearing your bra and panties."

Bev laughed, typing her response. "And if I am?"

His response surprised her. "Take a picture and send it to me."

"I don't think that's a good idea."

"Come on, bra and panties are nothing more than a bikini."

While Bev was thinking about what to do, Harry sent another message. "Come on, do it for me."

Instead of answering him, she posed, snapped her picture and sent it to him.

She blushed reading his message.

"You have a fantastic body. You look better than I thought you would. Thanks and goodnight."

***

Several days later when Bev's mom was surfing the Internet, her mouth fell open. It had to be a mistake. A picture of Bev in her underwear had been posted on the Internet?

SEND ME YOUR PICTURE
DISCUSSION QUESTIONS

A conversation may generate from the story. If it does not, the questions below are offered as a starting point for a discussion.

1. What dangers did Bev face when she sent Harry her picture?

2. Explain whether there are other dangers of having Bev's picture on the Internet.

3. What can Bev's mom do about her daughter's picture being on the Internet?

15

THE GRADUATION PARTY

Being a senior in high school meant parties. Lena Curtis and Teena Lewis were best friends, seniors, and popular. Every weekend they had received an invitation to a party.

The upcoming Saturday graduation party made Lena uncomfortable. They had been invited to a party, but they didn't know the boy giving it.

If Teena had concerns she had not voiced them. In addition, Teena volunteered to drive, but Lena was the designated driver.

Thinking about it, Lena should have asked her parents if she could drive to the party. But Lena knew why she had not asked them.

Her dad and mom would have demanded details. *"What is the name of the student giving the party? What are the address and telephone number of the party? Who are the chaperones?"*

Lena lacked information about the party's particulars and that meant her parents would not have given her permission to attend the party.

On Saturday, Teena picked Lena up. Approaching the address of the house, Lena felt uneasy. Teena parked the car and Lena asked, "Do you hear how loud the music is playing?"

"Take a chill pill. This is a party."

"I know, but if the music is that loud, I can guarantee there are no adult chaperones."

Teena didn't seem to care. She was busy looking at the car's lighted mirror, touching up her makeup.

"Let's go home." Lena suggested. "Better yet, why don't we go see the new movie we wanted to see?"

Teena glared at Lena. "Are you kidding?"

Lena tried one more time. "I think we should leave."

Rather than respond to Lena, Teena climbed out of the car and walked around the car. She stood beside the passenger's door and pulled it open.

"Let's go." Teena smiled. "This is what we've been waiting for—our senior year—parties—and having fun. Now, get out of the car."

Taking a deep breath, Lena climbed out. Before they reached the house, she said, "Listen, Teena, we need to stay together. Most of all, we came together. We leave together. Do you understand?"

"Whatever."

The closer they walked to the house, the louder the music boomed. The front door was open and the inside lighting was dim. Entering, Lena grabbed Teena by the arm.

"I don't see anyone we know. Can we go please?"

"What is wrong with you tonight? Give the party a chance. Let's get something to drink?"

Before Lena could answer, Teena sashayed off, leaving her alone at the door. Already Teena had forgotten what she had said about sticking together.

Lena tried adjusting her eyes to the dark room. She had no idea which direction Teena walked off to. She edged her way through the crowd and found where the drinks were being served.

"Where was Teena?" Lena thought.

Frustrated, worried and angry, she searched every room with care. Teena was not in any of them. Lena walked outside.

Lena fumed. Teena's car was gone. She bristled. "Damn her. She left me."

"Hey Lena." She turned around and felt relieved seeing a familiar face.

"How's it going?"

"Better, if I knew where Teena was? By any chance have you seen her?"

"Yeah, I saw her a few minutes ago leave with some dude."

Lena couldn't believe it. This is not the first time Teena's done this.

"Hey, are you okay?"

"It's just that I'm worried about Teena."

"Do you need a ride home?"

"I don't know. I should wait for Teena to return."

"Okay, but I think you should leave now. The buzz is that the neighbors called the police, and they'll probably arrive soon."

"What am I going to do?"

"I don't know, but if you want a ride, I'll take you home."

"Thanks, Billy." Lena hated leaving Teena, but what else could she do?

***

The next morning, Lena's telephone rang. "Hello."

"Lena, this is Mrs. Lewis." She paused. "Did Teena spend the night at your house last night?"

"No, ma'am."

Mrs. Lewis' voice was firm. "Didn't you go to the party together?"

Lena felt guilty. "Yes ma'am, but...." She cleared her throat. "She...she...I didn't see her leave the party, but someone saw her go off with some guy."

"What guy?"

"I don't know. I didn't see her when she left. I'm sorry I don't have more information." Through sobs she said, "I'm sorry."

THE GRADUATION PARTY
DISCUSSION QUESTIONS

A conversation may generate from the story. If it does not, the questions below are offered as a starting point for a discussion.

1. Explain why or why not Lena and Teena should have gone to the graduation party.

2. Do you believe Lena's parents would have been unreasonable wanting to know the name, address and telephone number of the person giving the party? Explain your answer.

3. What should Lena have done when she couldn't find Teena?

16

THE AMUSEMENT PARK

Robert Jones, Junior, nicknamed RJ paced back and forth. He and his friends, Chad and Fred had been looking forward to going to the amusement park. In two weeks, school would open and today was the last day for it.

Every time RJ heard a car in front of the house, he glanced out the window. He mumbled. *"Where are you mom?"* She should have been home thirty minutes ago.

RJ understood why he had to babysit his seven year old brother, Eric, after school, but it was times like this he wished both of his parents didn't work.

He thought, *"I hope mom comes home soon."* He picked up the ringing phone.

"Hello, RJ. This is mom. I…I'm sorry, but I'm going to be late. My relief called in sick. I have to work her shift until the supervisor finds someone else."

RJ ran his hand through his hair. "Mom, this is just great!"

Silence followed his outburst. "What am I supposed to do?"

His mother's voice was soft. "I know how much you've been looking forward to going to the amusement park…but, your dad's airplane doesn't arrive until seven o'clock and…." She paused.

"I'll tell you what, you can still go, but you'll have to take your little brother."

RJ's voice was louder than he intended. "Mom, there's no way I'm taking Eric with me."

His mom's voice was firm. "If you want to go, you'll have to take him."

RJ took his time answering. He mumbled. "Okay. I'll take him, but mom, talk to him. Tell him he has to listen to me."

"Okay. Put him on the phone."

Smiling and nodding his head, Eric said, "I'll behave."

RJ hung up the phone and turned to his brother. "Okay, let's go."

They reached the car and Eric asked, "Can I sit up front with you?"

"This is what I'm talking about." RJ took a deep breath. "We haven't left the driveway, and already you're bugging me. No you can't sit upfront."

RJ fumed. "Get in the back and make sure you fasten your seatbelt."

In front of the amusement park, Chad and Fred stood, watching RJ and Eric walk toward them.

Chad smirked, "Why is Eric with you?"

RJ rolled his eyes. "Don't ask, it's a long story, but he won't give us any trouble."

He glanced down at Eric. "Isn't that right?"

Before Eric answered RJ grabbed him by the arm and pulled him into the roller coaster line.

While waiting their turn, Chad whispered. "Do you think Eric can ride the roller coaster?"

RJ shrugged. He grabbed Eric and took him to the front of the line where the man-in-charge of the ride stood.

"Excuse me. What are the rules for riding the roller coaster?"

The man pointed. "Everyone's height has to meet or exceed the measurement guide."

Eric stood with his back up against the post. He wasn't tall enough, even with him standing on his tiptoes.

"Sir, can you make an exception." RJ pleaded. "This is my little brother and …."

The man shook his head and pointed to the sign, his voice gruff.

"You see the rules. If he isn't tall enough, he doesn't ride."

RJ sulked, strolling back to his friends, Eric following behind him.

He explained. "Eric can't ride. He's not tall enough."

RJ stooped down and looked at his brother. "Listen, Eric, wait right here by the fence. When I get off the roller coaster you can ride whatever you want. Okay?"

Eric pouted, but agreed. He watched RJ, Chad and Fred get on the ride.

Getting off the roller coaster, the boys laughed and talked with excitement. They exclaimed about the speed and all the dips and curves.

"Hey, let's get back in line and do it again." Fred suggested.

"You guys go ahead. I promised Eric I'd take him on something he can." Walking away, he turned and said, "I'll catch up with you later."

RJ strolled over to the fence where he had left Eric standing. He wasn't there. He rushed over to the man running the roller coaster.

"Excuse me! Do you remember the little boy who was with me?"

"Yeah. What about him?"

"Well, did you notice where he might have gone?"

"Do I look like a babysitter? Once you left with the kid, I never saw him again."

RJ ran over to several nearby rides and yelled, "Eric, Eric."

Chad and Fred heard RJ yelling. They stepped out of the roller coaster line and hurried over to him.

In unison, they asked, "What's going on?"

"I can't find Eric. Will you help me search for him?"

They agreed to meet back at the roller coaster in thirty minutes. They walked off in different directions. When they returned to the meeting place, no one had found him.

RJ pulled out his cell phone and called his mom.

THE AMUSEMENT PARK
DISCUSSION QUESTIONS

A conversation may generate from the story. If it does not, the questions below are offered as a starting point for a discussion.

1. What other options did RJ's mother have other than have RJ babysit his little brother?

2. What other instructions should RJ's mother given her sons other than telling Ronnie to listen to his big brother?

3. What should RJ have done to make sure his brother was safe while he and his friends rode the roller coaster?

REFERENCES

The stories in this book are fictitious, but I suggest anyone reading this book might consult other venues when addressing these difficult issues. Individuals may seek additional information and guidance when having a discussion about the stories from the following:

1. The local police department have trained and skilled professionals who can discuss ways to protect children.

2. School counselors are educated and trained to address issues discussed in this book.

3. Libraries are filled with books regarding the safety of children. Several helpful books on the subject are:

   - Are you a good stranger? Author, Susan Nichols
   - Stranger Danger and Safety. Author, Dr. Rick Collingwood

4. The Internet is full of resourceful information on the subject of child safety. Several helpful Internet sites are:

- www.amw.com
- www.kids.gov

www.ingramcontent.com/pod-product-compliance
Lightning Source LLC
Chambersburg PA
CBHW071410170626
46811CB00003B/1332